Machines

By Ann Morris   Photographs by Ken Heyman

 GoodYearBooks

This machine goes
up, up, up.

This machine goes
round, round, round.

This machine goes
chop, chop, chop.

This machine goes
down, down, down.

This machine goes
crunch, crunch, crunch.

These machines go
crash, bam, boom!